W9-CUF-882

the
Dream Book

the Dream Book

MARGARET WISE BROWN

Illustrated by
RICHARD FLOETHE

A DELL PICTURE YEARLING BOOK

Published by
Dell Publishing
a division of
Bantam Doubleday Dell Publishing Group, Inc.
666 Fifth Avenue
New York, New York 10103

ISBN: 0-440-40567-X
Reprinted by arrangement with WaterMark, Incorporated
Printed in the United States of America
October 1991

10 9 8 7 6 5 4 3 2 1

LBM

About the author and artist . . .

MARGARET WISE BROWN published well over one hundred books in her short lifetime, including *Goodnight Moon, The Runaway Bunny,* and *David's Little Indian.* A number of stories that remained unpublished at her death have since been published, including *Four Fur Feet.* Miss Brown was born in New York, and graduated from Hollins College in Virginia. For three years she was editor of children's books at William R. Scott, Inc., Publisher.

RICHARD FLOETHE was born in Essen, Germany and studied art in Dortmund, Munich and Viemar. When he arrived in the United States, he worked for a short time as a commercial artist. He has won many awards for his children's illustrations. Several of his prints are in the collections of the New York Public Library and the Metropolitan Museum of Art.

Sleep little squirrel and dream your dream
Of nuts that fall
And a lima bean

Sleep little rabbit the carrot grows
All through the garden and under your nose

Sleep little horse the day is over
Endless fields of sweet green clover
Blow about your hoofs

For everyone a world is a wish
For the child the rabbit and the fish
Call it a wish or call it a dream
Of a world that could be as it can seem
Towards such a world first comes the dream

The little bee dreams of hives of honey

The soldier dreams of something funny

The little boy dreams of hammers and nails
And marbles and tops and boats with sails

The little girl dreams of dolls and flowers
And horses and bunnies that hop for hours

The fish must dream of more and more water
Of a lobster's niece and a flounder's daughter

The little bird dreams of an endless song
Sung in the branches all night long

The little mouse dreams of another mouse
And living all warm in a tiny house

For everyone in dream will stray
Hours of the night and some of the day
Think of the world as it can seem
Towards such a world first comes the dream

Night comes on without a sound
A soft dark shadow all around
Bright eyes and flowers all must close
The child's the rabbit's and the rose

Dreaming child what you shall see
Deep in sleep
Might some day be.